KT-131-776

This book belongs to:

....

....

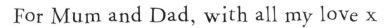

For Mum and Dad, with all my love x

A NEW BURLINGTON BOOK
The Old Brewery
6 Blundell Street
London N7 9BH

Editor: Ruth Symons
Designer: Bianca Lucas
Managing Editor: Victoria Garrard
Design Manager: Anna Lubecka

Copyright © QED Publishing 2013

First published in the UK in 2013 by QED Publishing
Part of The Quarto Group

All rights reserved. No part of this publication may be reproduced, stored
in a retrieval system, or transmitted in any form or by any means, electronic,
mechanical, photocopying, recording, or otherwise, without the prior
permission of the publisher, nor be otherwise circulated in any form
of binding or cover other than that in which it is published and without
a similar condition being imposed on the subsequent purchaser.

A catalogue record for this book is available from the British Library.

ISBN 978 1 78171 359 4

Printed in China

SQUIRREL'S BUSY DAY

by Lucy Barnard

NB
NEW BURLINGTON

It was autumn, so Squirrel decided to spend the day collecting acorns.

He set off down the path with his old red trolley.

Squirrel hadn't gone far when
Rabbit bounced out of the bushes.

"Morning, Squirrel!" Rabbit said.
"Do you want to play chase
through the leaves?"

"I can't today,
I'm too busy,"
Squirrel said,
and he hurried along.

Soon, Squirrel met his friend Mouse.

"Do you want to come and play in my nest?" squeaked Mouse.

"Not right now, I don't have time," Squirrel said, and he rushed off.

Squirrel had lots of acorns
in his trolley when he
passed Badger's den.

"Hello, Squirrel," Badger called out.
"How are you today?"

"No time to talk, I'm gathering acorns!"
Squirrel said, and he scurried away.

Squirrel's trolley was nearly full
when he met Owl and Fox.

"Hello**OOOOO**,
Squirrel,"
hooted Owl.

"It's a lovely day,"
barked Fox.
"Come and play!"

"I don't have time today, I'm in a hurry,"
puffed Squirrel, tugging at his trolley.

Huff!
Puff!

At last,
Squirrel's trolley was full—
and very, very heavy.

As he heaved it to the top of
a steep hill, he heard a loud...

CRACK!

The handle had
snapped
off!

The broken trolley
rolled down the hill,
hit a stone and...

CRASH!

The acorns went flying.

Just then the leaves behind Squirrel rustled.

"I heard
a noise,"
hooted Owl.

"Are you okay?"
Fox asked.

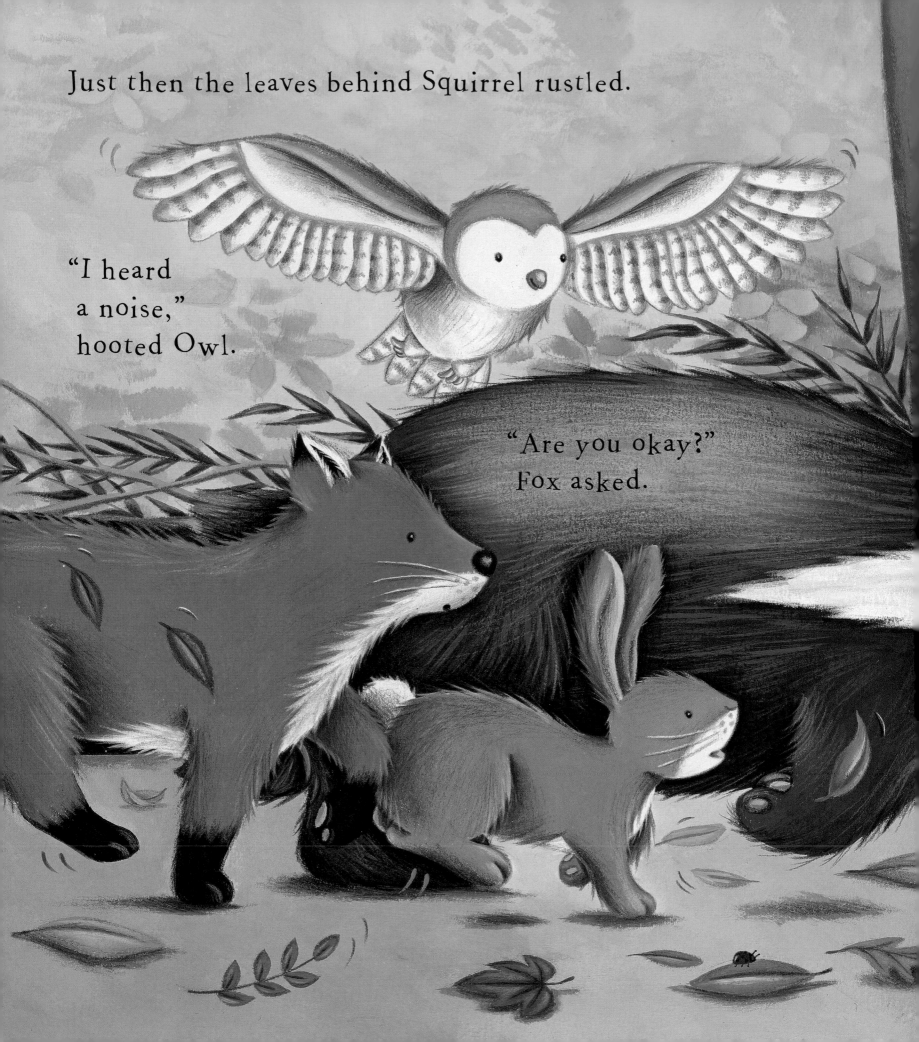

"My acorns have gone everywhere,"
Squirrel said. "I'll never find them all!"

"We'll help you," squeaked Mouse.
"Together, we'll find them in no time."

And that's just what they did...

Mouse found **one** under a big leaf.

Fox found **two** beside some mushrooms.

Owl found **three** in a group of fir cones.

Badger found **four** behind a mossy log.

And Rabbit found **five** on some spiky grass.

The animals piled all the acorns into the trolley.

Then they helped Squirrel push the trolley back home.

"I'm sorry I didn't stop to play,"
Squirrel said. "You've all been so kind."

"That's what friends are for!"
Badger replied with a smile.

"Friends are also for playing
chase with," laughed Squirrel,
as he raced off through the leaves.

"Catch me if you can!"

NEXT STEPS

Show the children the cover again. Could they have guessed what the story is about? Does the title give them a clue?

When you have read the story together, ask the children why Squirrel was too busy to play with his friends. Why do they think Squirrel was collecting so many acorns?

Squirrel was too busy to spend time with his friends, but they helped him when he needed them. Working together, the animals found all of the acorns. Ask the children about their friends. When have they helped a friend?

Talk to the children about the other characters in the story. Have they ever seen those animals before? Ask the children to draw their favourite animal from the story.

Act out the story. Perhaps one of the children could collect balls, toys or balloons instead of acorns. Do any of them have a cart or a trolley like Squirrel's?

At the end of the story, the animals play chase. What games do the children like to play with their friends?